NICK JR.

DORA the EXPLORER®

DORA'S SNOWY FOREST ADVENTURE

adapted by Laury ᴇrnardt
illustrated by Robert Roper

Ready-to-Read

Simon Spotlight/Nick Jr.
New York   London   Toronto   Sydney

Based on the TV series *Dora the Explorer*® as seen on Nick Jr.®

SIMON SPOTLIGHT
An imprint of Simon & Schuster Children's Publishing Division
1230 Avenue of the Americas, New York, New York 10020
Manufactured in the United States of America
6 8 10 9 7 5
Library of Congress Cataloging-in-Publication Data
Silverhardt, Lauryn.
Dora's snowy forest adventure / by Lauryn Silverhardt ; illustrated by Robert Roper. — 1st ed.
p. cm. — (Ready-to-read ; #18)
"Based on the TV series Dora the Explorer as seen on Nick Jr."—Copyright p.
ISBN-13: 978-1-4169-5865-9
ISBN-10: 1-4169-5865-7
I. Roper, Robert. II. Dora the explorer (Television program) III. Title.
PZ7.S58585Dor 2008
[E]—dc22
2007037837

Hi! I am  DORA . I am going

to read a story.

Do you like  BOOKS ?

Me too!

Once upon a time there was a

SNOW PRINCESS

who lived in a Magic 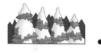 .

SNOWY FOREST

"Look, ," says 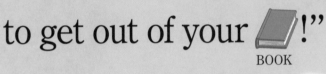.

DORA BOOTS

"Someone is trying

to get out of your !"

BOOK

"Hi! My name is .

SNOW FAIRY

I need to find the

SNOW PRINCESS and save

the Magic SNOWY FOREST."

"A  waved

WITCH

her

MAGIC WAND

and locked the

SNOW PRINCESS

in a 🗼 .

TOWER

With the  gone,

the Magic

is starting to melt!"

Then  adds,

SNOW FAIRY

"If the

SNOW PRINCESS

smiles into a magic CRYSTAL ,

it will start to SNOW again!"

BOOTS and I will help

save the SNOW PRINCESS .

Who do we ask for help

when we don't know where

to go?

Yeah,  !

 says we need to go

across the  ,
ICY OCEAN

past the  ,
SNOWY HILLS

and through the .
DARK CAVE

The
PIRATE PIGGIES

will take us across the
ICY OCEAN

in their  .
PIRATE SHIP

Watch out for the !
SEA SNAKE

We made it!

Now we need to find a way

down the  .

SNOWY HILLS

"Look! Maybe that girl can help us," says  .
BOOTS

"Hi! My name is 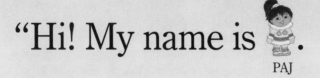.
PAJ

I can take you to the !
DARK CAVE

Jump on my !"
DOG SLED

Thanks, .

That was great!

Now I see the .

DARK CAVE

Come on!

We made it through

the .

DARK CAVE

Look! I see the !

TOWER

Hooray! We made it

to the .
TOWER

I see the !
WITCH

We need to hurry.

We found the  !
SNOW PRINCESS

But the  cast a spell
WITCH

on her!

She cannot  .
SMILE

Maybe if we all

SMILE

into the magic ,

CRYSTAL

we can break the spell.

 with us!

SMILE

One, two, three– !

SMILE

Yay! We did it!

The  is free!

SNOW PRINCESS

The Magic

SNOWY FOREST

is saved!

Thank you for helping us

 into the magic .

SMILE   CRYSTAL

We broke the spell!